Disney STITCH!

YUMI TSUKIRINO

STITCH

The 626th experiment made by Dr. Jumba. Has the brain of a super computer and a great sense of smell, amazing night vision, good hearing, and uncanny strength. However, he causes all sorts of trouble because he can't distinguish between right and wrong!

YUNA

An incredibly energetic little girl living with Grandma on the Okinawan island of Izayoi. She is especially good at karate. As the heir of the "Chitama-style Karate Dojo," she teaches karate to the students.

Yuna's grandmother.
She knows an awful lot about Izayoi's traditions, culture, and nature. In addition to those on Izayoi, she's also friends with yokai spirits throughout the world.

STITCH!
DR. JUMBA
A self-proclaimed evil scientist and Stitch's creator. He came to Izayoi with Pleakley in search of Stitch.
PLEAKLEY
A self-proclaimed leading Earth expert, he is carrying out his role of gathering information for the Galactic Council. He came to Izayoi along with Dr. Jumba to look for Stitch. He loves to cosplay.
KIJIMUNAA
A yokai taking the form of a young boy who lives in the forests of Izayoi. He is supposedly the greatest yokai on the island, but he's an incredible coward and tends to keep to himself. He rarely ventures out beyond the forest.
KOUJI
A sixth grader attending the same elementary school as Yuna. He acts like the leader of the kids of the island and is always throwing his weight around.
PIKO
Kouji's younger sister. Well known for her sarcasm an a sore loser.

CONTENTS

Stitch Meets Yuna! 5
Stitch Goes to See the Chitama Stone! 15
Stitch Makes Juice! 24
Stitch Goes Fishing! 30
Stitch... Can Be Good?! 38
Stitch Finds Treasure(?!) 46
Stitch Enters the Costume Festival! 56
Stitch Does Laundry! 63
Stitch Helps Taro! 71
Yuna Forgets Her Homework! 79
Stitch Meets Kijimunaa! 87
Stitch Is a Super Star Skater?! 94

Special Edition: Lilo and Stitch

Stitch Makes a Cake 103
Find the Mysterious Butterfly! 112
Stitch Is a Talented Artist?! 120
Let's Take a Bath! 127
Happiness from the Snow Machine?! 135
Operation: Nani's Date! 143
Treasure Hunting at the Beach! 151
Find Scrump! 158
Seed of the Happiness Flower 167

STITCH MEETS YUNA!
This is the alien "Stitch," created by Dr. Jumba.
He is currently involved in a high-speed chase on his space scooter!
STOP!
EYAHAHA-HAHA!
ME GENIUS!
All of a sudden, a space storm rolled through and sucked him up.
WAHA-HAHA!

He landed on "Izayoi Island"!!
WHERE THIS?
GRRGGGRRUUU
SO HUNGRY!!
BAM
GRRGGGG
GRUMMBLE
GRGH
STARE
WHAT'S THAT?
IT HAS HUGE EARS AND A BLUE BODY.
POKE POKE POKE
GRAWR!
SO HUNGRY!!!
WAAAAAGH!

HMM, SO YOU'RE STITCH, HUH?
YEP! STITCH!
I'M YUNA!
I WAS ON MY WAY TO GO PICK SOME MANGOES,
SO WHY DONTCHA COME ALONG IF YOU'RE HUNGRY? ♡
MANGO?
HEHE... THIS TREE HERE HAS SOME DEEEEELICIOUS MANGOES.
THIS IS MY SECRET SPOT, Y'KNOW.
WAIT A SEC!
スル SHTK
スル SHTK
プチ PLUCK
プチ PLUCK

AWRIGHT!
HERE YA GO!
くん SNIFF くん SNIFF くん SNIFF
ザラ～ BADUM
ガッ SCARF
ガッ SCARF
ガッ SCARF
ガッ SCARF
さっ PEW
HEY...!
もぐ MUNCH
KICK
もぐ MUNCH
...
もぐ MUNCH
もぐ MUNCH
どーん BANG

READ THIS WAY
BUM BUM BUM
SCARF
SCARF
SCARF
YOU LITTLE-!
HAIYA!
KA!
WHA?!
WHAT YOU DOING?!
THAT'S WHAT I'D LIKE TO SAY!!
WHAT A RUDE LITTLE BEAST, NOT EVEN SAYING THANK YOU!
I'M NOT GOING TO STAND FOR THAT KIND OF ATTI-TUDE!

SHAKE
わな
わな
SHAKE
YOU... LITTLE!
PLINK
タネ。
PEEEEEEW★
SPIT
SPIT
プイッ
PAH!
FINE, I'M OUTTA HERE.
GAH
SCARF
ガッ
SCARF
ガッ

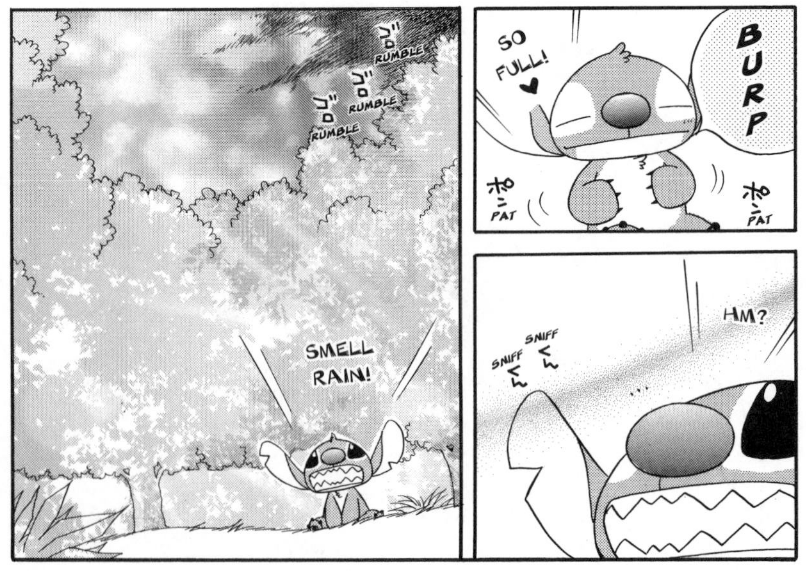
BURP
SO FULL! ♥
ポン
PAT
ポン
PAT
ゴロ
RUMBLE
ゴロ
RUMBLE
ゴロ
RUMBLE
SMELL RAIN!
HM?
SNIFF
くん
SNIFF
くん

GAAAH, WHO THE HECK DOES HE THINK HE IS?
プン
GRUMBLE
プン
GRUMBLE
I'M SO MAD!
HUH?
IT'S RAINING!
ポツ
PLOP
ポツ
PLOP
サァァ…
SHAAAA
だっ
STEP
I GOTTA HURRY!
ピカ
CRACK
ゴロゴロゴロゴロ
RUMMMMMMMBLE
NO WAY!
I HATE THUNDER!
バシャ
SPLASH
バシャ
SPLASH
ザー
SHAAAAAAA

TRIP
EYAGH!
SHAAAAAA
CRACK
OW-OW-OW.
BOOOOOOOM
ZZZZZZZZZT
CREEEEEEEEK
FWOOOOM
WHA...?

AAAAAAAAAAAAAH!!!
ドドオオオ
DOOOOOOOOO
ガ
GRAB
グググ…
NNNNG
STITCH STRONG!
HE-HE-HE.
STITCH!!

* IN THIS STORY, "COUSINS" MEANS

STITCH GOES TO SEE THE CHITAMA STONE!
Yuna and Stitch have become the best of friends.
Now, they're sleeping in Yuna's room.
NNNG
KICK
ゴロン
WRIGGLE
ムクッ
PLOP
どすん
BADUM
...
NNNG
GNNG!
ZZZZ
SO... HEAVY!
じたばた
WRIGGLE

GAH
GET OFF!
KICK
OWW?
GGGGGGRUBLE
GRRUGLE
GRRRUUU
YUNA! SO HUNGRY! WAKE UP!!!
GRAGH!
HEY!
QUID-DIT!
GOOD MORNING, GRANDMA.
YAAAAWN!
GOOD MORNING, YUNA.
WELL, LET'S SIT DOWN FOR BREAK-FAST.
OOOH, BREAK-FAST!
Grandma
Yuna's grandmother

READ THIS WAY

SNAP
UAAGH!
PLINK
YOU HAVE AWFUL MANNERS, STITCH!
AAAH!
NO WAY! YOU'RE EATING EVERY-THING!
ガッ SCARF
ガッ SCARF
ガッ SCARF
YOU ATE MY FOOD, TOO!
ガッ SCARF
ガッ SCARF
ガッ SCARF
ガッ SCARF
ゴクゴク GULP
ゴクーッ GULP

STITCH, AWESOME!
くる SPIN
くる SPIN
くる SPIN
EYAHA-HAHAHA!
SLIP
OOPS!
ガシャ〜ン☆ CRASH
STIIIIIIIITCH!
WELL, IT WAS A NICE BREAK-FAST.
CRASH
CRASH
CRASH
GET OVER HERE, STITCH.
I WANT TO SHOW A NAUGHTY LITTLE GUY LIKE YOU SOMETHING NICE.
ズン DRAG
ズン DRAG
WHA? WHHH-HHY?
LOOK!
ざっ FWISH
?

ばーーーーーーーーん!
TAAAAAADAAAAAH!
THIS IS THE "CHITAMA STONE," AN AMAAAAZING STONE THAT WILL GRANT YOU ANY WISH!
WISH!
ANY-THING!
STITCH WILL BE STRON-GEST
IN THE UNIVERSE!
No 1 !!
SPROING
ばっ

BOOMF
YEP, LOOKS LIKE YOU GOT DENIED SINCE YOU'RE NOT BEING GOOD.
HA HA!
STITCH IS GOOD! STITCH DO GOOD THINGS!
YUNA GET TIRED BY WALKING HOME!
HEY!
STITCH GIVE YOU PIGGYBACK RIDE!
GRAB
AAACH!
POOOOOOOING
THE BRANCH-ES ARE HITTING ME!
HOP
HOP
OWW!
JUMP
JUMP
SHF
SHF
SHF
AAAAAAH!

ボロ〜〜… OWWW
IS STITCH GOOD NOW?
NNG... SURE, OKAY.
わく PANT
わく PANT
BUT IT'S STILL TOO SOON TO GRANT YOUR WISH.
しょぼん… SLUNK
STITCH ...
BUT, IF YOU DO GOOD DEEDS,
IT'LL DEFINITELY COME TRUE! ♡
STITCH HUNGRY!
SCARF ガッ
SCARF ガッ
CLAAAANG ガシャン
MY FLAN!
WHAT?
STIIIIIIIII-ITCH!

GRRR-
RMBLE
STARE
STITCH, YOU'RE GONNA CATCH A COLD.
YOU SHOULDN'T SLEEP LIKE THAT.
コチョ POKE
コチョ～ POKE
STITCH MAKES JUICE!

ガバァ
CHEW
SO HUNGRY!!
WHAA?? AGAIN?!

THAT'S BECAUSE YOU DIDN'T GET BACK BY SNACK TIME.
WHAT WAS TODAY'S SNACK?
TODAY'S SNACK WAS FRUIT JUICE.
IT WAS MADE BY YOURS TRULY!

READ THIS WAY
LATELY, I'VE BEEN INTO MAKING MY OWN ORIGINAL CONCOCTIONS. HMM... WHAT'LL I MAKE TODAY?
GRRRRR
RUMBLE
GURGLE

HMM...
I'LL TRY THESE THREE FRUITS!
キョロ GLANCE
キョロ GLANCE
VRRRRRRR
OOH! ♡

MUNCH
SCARF
SCARF
MUNCH
SCARF

THE FLAVOR NEEDS A LITTLE SOMETHING.
BURP

POP
カパッ
トパポー
SLOOOOSH
♫
SHAKE
SHAKE
HEY, WHAT'RE YOU DOING??
MILK
SOY SAUCE
EUGH! MILK, FISH, AND SOY SAUCE?!
CUT IT OUT!
VRR
VRR
VRR
MILK
♪
♫
YUNA!
ACK!
G... GRANDMA!
?
YOU MUSTN'T WASTE FOOD!!
GLARE
DRINK. IT. ALL.

BOOM
WHEN GRANDMA'S STEAMED, SHE GETS REALLY SCARY, Y'KNOW. WE BETTER DRINK IT!
ヒソ ヒソ
PSST PSST
...
...
ROCK, PAPER, SCIS-SORS.
ROCK
SHOOT!
PAPER
EYAHAHA-HAHA! STITCH WINS!
THIS STINKS!
FWOOOOOOM
EYEUGH
フル フル
TREMBLE
WELL, I LOST.
BLECH!!
ゴクゴク—ッ!!
GUUUUUUULP

DIS... DISGUSTING... ABSOLUTELY DISGUSTING!
くらくら〜
SO WOOZY
HEEHEE, YUNA LOSE!!
BUT!
BUT!
I KNOW ... I'LL PRETEND IT'S DELI-CIOUS.
D... DELICIOUS!
THIS IS WONDER-FUL!
I'LL TRICK STITCH AND MAKE HIM DRINK IT!
YOU SHOULD TRY IT, STITCH!
STITCH DRINK, TOO!
ゴクゴクーッ
GLUG
GLUG
YES!!
PAAAH
SO GOOD!
HUH?!

READ THIS WAY

MAYBE THAT FIRST TASTE WAS JUST MY IMAGINATION?
YUNA A GENIUS! AMAZING!
CLAP
CLAP
OH YEAH...? HEHEHE!
HERE GOES!
GLUG
GLUG
...
SHAKE
SHAKE
YOU LIAR!! IT'S DISGUSTING!!
THUD
THUD
THUD
THUD
THUD
HUH? WHAT'S WRONG? IT'S REALLY TASTY!
Yuna and the alien, Stitch.
HOLD UP!!!
STITCH AND YUNA'S TASTEBUDS ARE DIFFERENT!!
Apparently they have a different sense of taste...

STIIIITCH, YOU ATE MY SNACK AGAIN, DIDN'T YOU?!
HM?
THIS IS THE THIRD DAY IN A ROW!
AND TODAY WAS FLAN, MY FAVORITE!!
ワナ SHAKE
ワナ SHAKE
ワナ SHAKE
STITCH GOES FISHING!
I WON'T FORGIVE YOU, STITCH! YOU BETTER APOLOGIZE!
ドドドドドーッ
THUD
THUD
AAAAAAAAH!

DASH
How-ever…
They had a foot race.
HE'S FAST!
Rock climbing.
PBBT!
BLEEEEEH!
HAH
HAH
HAH
HOLD UP, YOU!
Aerial combat.
SHT SHT SHT
HEY, WAIT!
WAIT UP!
THERE'S JUST NO WAY FOR ME TO WIN IN A BATTLE OF STRENGTH.
HOW CAN I BEAT STITCH?
AND MAKE HIM SAY HE'S SORRY?
HA!
HA!
HA!
HA!
EYAHAHA-HAHA!
STITCH TOO STRONG! HEHEHE!

I GOT IT!
HEY STITCH, HOW ABOUT A FISHING COMPETITION?
FISHING?
FISHING IS WHEN YOU PUT A STRING ON A WOODEN ROD AND CATCH FISH.
WOOD IN ROD?
IF YOU WIN, I'LL HAND OVER MY SNACK EVERY DAY!
AND IF YOU LOSE, YOU BETTER APOLOGIZE.
OOH! YUNA'S SNACK!♡ OKAY, OKAY!
URGH!
STITCH THINKS THERE'S NO WAY HE'LL LOSE.
OH, WHATEVER!
ALRIGHT, FIRST TO CATCH A FISH WINS!
HERE'S YOUR FISHING ROD.
OK!!

し――――ん…
SILENCE
LIKE I THOUGHT, HE'S ALREADY BORED.
SHUFFLE, SHUFFLE
TOSS
YAAAAAAWN
PLUNK
GOT ON!
OKAY, NOW MY VICTORY!
ざっぱーーん
SPLASH

ポテッ
PLOP
HUH?
AN OCTOPUS?
SPLOOOOSH
AAAAAGH!
EWW, I CAN'T SEE A THING!
チャぽん
SPLASH
EYAHA-HAHAHA! YUNA ALL BLACK!
CHORTLE
CHORTLE
AND THE OCTOPUS GOT AWAY, TOO! HOW ROTTEN!
NOW STITCH CATCH ONE!
キィ
WOOD
CRACK

GRAB
CHK
SWOOOOOOSH!!
FWEEEE
BADUM!
HEHE
AAAAH, I LOST!
PLUP
PLUP

HMPH... THIS STINKS.
RUMBLE
YUNA HUNGRY!
I GIVE YOU FISH! EAT!
WHAT, REALLY??
YOU ACTUALLY CAN BE NICE, HUH, STITCH?
THANKS!
ぱっ GRAB
MUNCH
OKAY, TIME TO EAT! ♡
AWWWWWW!
...
DROOOOL
STIIIITCH!
ぴょん SPROING
STITCH HUNGRY, TOO!
...

POP

I HOPE THAT DAD'S JOB IS GOING WELL.
I WANT HIM TO COME BACK SOON.
STITCH... CAN BE GOOD?!
DID YOU DO A GOOD JOB WITH THE LAUNDRY?
GRANDMA!
YEP!
BUT THIS IS DAD'S FROM WHEN HE WAS LITTLE, SO IT'S A LITTLE RATTY.
ガサッ
KSSST
HM?
HEY, STITCH IS TEARING UP THE GOYA FIELDS AGAIN!
ガサ
PLUCK
ゴソ
RIP
ガサ
PLUCK
ガサ
PLUCK

WELL, WHAT CAN YOU DO...
CUT IT OUT, STITCH!
MUNCH
MUNCH
SNAP
SNAP
CRACK
CHUCK
OUTTA HERE!
PWOOOM
CLANG
CLANG
AUGH, THE EISA VEST!
HM?

WHAT WRONG, YUNA?
DON'T 'WHAT'S WRONG' ME!
DIDN'T YOU SEE THE EISA VEST FALL?
APOLOGIZE, RIGHT NOW!
YOU LITTLE...!
TOO BUSY NOW.
MUNCH
MUNCH
MUNCH
BANG
APOLOGIZE!
WHIFF
WHEN YOU DO BAD THINGS, YOU APOLOGIZE!
ISN'T THAT WHAT I'M ALWAYS TELLING YOU?

CAW
NO! DAD'S EISA VEST!
CAW
OH NO, YUNA!
HUH?
CAW
HOLD UP!
DAD? EISA?
WHAT'LL I DO?
THOSE ARE THE CLOTHES THAT YUNA'S FATHER WEARS AT THE FESTIVAL.
THEY'RE VERY IMPORTANT.
I...I'M GONNA GO LOOK FOR THAT BIRD AND MAKE HIM GIVE IT BACK.
GLARE
THIS IS ALL YOUR FAULT, STITCH, SO YOU'RE GOING, TOO!

YUNA, UP! THE BIRD!!
THE BIRD'S NEST!
HMM, IT WANTED THE EISA VEST AS MA-TERIAL FOR THE NEST...
GROOOOOAN
GIVE BACK EISA!! BIRD!!
WHA?!
N... NO, YOU CAN'T DO THAT!
BANG
BANG
THE NEST WILL FALL.

TUMBLE
ACK!
THE NEST!
HK
DASH
CATCH
HAAAH
I MADE IT!
OH, CHICKS!
CHIRP
CHIRP
CHIRP
HUH?
GREAT!
OH, HERE'S DAD'S EISA VEST!

THESE LITTLE CHICKS MUST MISS THEIR PARENTS.
WHAT SHOULD WE DO?
CHIRP
CHIRP

GRAB
HEY!
WHAT ARE YOU DOING??

ぴょん
BUM
SWING
SWING
SWING
SWING
だ
JUMP
...
どん
BADUM
OH, YOU PUT THE NEST IN THE NEIGHBOR-ING TREE!

READ THIS WAY
YOU DID PRETTY GOOD THERE. I'M STARTING TO THINK TWICE ABOUT YOU, STITCH!
I'M REALLY SURPRISED!
YUNA ...
STITCH DO GOOD!
EHE-HE
GRIN
HAHA! LET'S GO HOME AND GET SOMETHING TO EAT!
SO HUUUU-UNGRY!
HA!
GRAAAA
IT WON'T BE TOO LONG UNTIL YOUR WISH IS GRANTED.
REALLY?! YUNA!
HAHAHA! YOU STILL HAVE A LOT OF GOOD DEEDS TO DO!
DO YOUR BEST, STITCH!

STITCH FINDS TREASURE(?!)

READ THIS WAY

WHO'S YOUR FRIEND, STITCH?
THIS YUNA! SHE'S OHANA.
I'M YUNA ...
BOW...
GREETINGS, I AM PLEAKLEY, THE LEADING EXPERT IN EARTH RESEARCH.
GAHAHA
AND I AM DR. JUMBA, AN EVIL SCIENTIST AND STITCH'S CREATOR.
THAT MEANS ...
I GUESS YOU'RE STITCH'S MOM AND DAD!
...
MOM? DAD?!
HAHAHA! NOW THAT'S THE FIRST TIME I'VE BEEN CALLED THAT!
LET'S TRY AUNT AND UNCLE INSTEAD!
NICE TO MEET YOU, YUNA.
NICE TO MEET YOU, TOO.

YOU KNOW, THIS IZAYOI IS A BEAUTIFUL ISLAND.
THERE ARE TONS OF UNIQUE THINGS TO SEE!
I KNOW, RIGHT? THERE ARE JUST TONS OF RARE AND BEAUTIFUL THINGS.
I'LL SHOW YA AROUND!
REALLY?? I'LL GO! I'LL GO!
AH, YES, IT SEEMS LIKE THERE WILL BE A LOT OF RESEARCH MATERIAL TO BE HAD.
ALL RIGHT, OFF WE GO!
C'MON STITCH, LET'S GO.
BUT!
STITCH HUNGRYYYY
And then...
OH, THESE MOSQUITOES ARE ADORABLE!
BZZZ
COME HERE, LITTLE GUYS!
ASIA-PACIFIC MOSQUITOES...!
OH!

READ
THIS
WAY

LOOK OVER HERE, ANTS!
THEY'RE MARCHING ALONG IN LITTLE LINES.
MARCH
MARCH
MARCH
HEY YUNA, LOOK, LOOK!
IT'S AN ASIA-PACIFIC HERMIT CRAB. WOOOOW!
IF YOU DIG AROUND IN THE UNDERWATER SAND, YOU'LL FIND A TON.
REALLY ??
I'M GOING DIGGING!
OOOH, I'M SO HAPPY!
PLEAKLEY IS... AN INTERESTING PERSON.
GREAT!
OOOH, THERE ARE SO MANY!
WELL, HE IS THE SELF-PROCLAIMED LEADING EARTH EXPERT.
YAAAAWN!
PAT
PAT

HEY, LET'S GO TO THE FOREST NEXT!
THERE ARE A LOT OF UNIQUE THINGS TO SEE IN THE FOREST...
OOOH! SHINY, SHINY!
HM?

LOOK! IT'S A PRETTY LITTLE GEM!
OOH!
A GEM??
THAT'S A MINERAL I'VE NEVER SEEN BE-FORE.
SO GEMS LIKE THIS CAN BE FOUND HERE? THIS BEACH IS AMAZING!

LET'S DIG UP SOME MORE EARTH GEMS!
YES, IT'S ALL ON YOU, STITCH.
OK!

BEWARE OF JELLYFISH
HMM... OH!

NNG
SNAP
WAIT! STITCH! NO!
SHFT
SHFT
SHFT
OH, HERE'S ONE!
AND ANOTHER!
SHFT
SHFT
SHFT
SHFT
...
BUT... THESE ARE JUST SHARDS OF GLASS...
DO ALIENS THINK THESE ARE SPECIAL?

どさっ!
DUMP
HEY, DON'T JUST BRING ALL THIS INTO MY ROOM!
PI PI PI PI
WELL, WELL... WHAT KIND OF MINERALS ARE THESE? IT MUST BE A NEW VARIETY!
YOU DON'T WANT THESE, YUNA?
I DON'T NEED THIS STUFF!
HM, WHAT'S THIS?! THIS IS JUST SIMPLE GLASS??
G... GLASS??
THAT'S RIGHT. SHARDS OF BOT-TLES AND OTH-ER STUFF GETS GROUND DOWN AND ROUNDED BY WAVES.

READ
THIS
WAY

B... BUT I THOUGHT IT WAS A NEW VARIETY OF MINERAL.
AND WE PICKED UP SO MANY, TOO.
BUT THEY REALLY ARE PRETTY! ♡
HEY, THAT'S RIGHT.
JUMBA, LET ME BORROW THIS.
SHUFFLE
ガサ
ゴソ
RATTLE
ビビビビ
ZZT
ZZT
ZZT
ぐにゃあ～～っ
VWOOOO
ビビビビ
ZZZZT
OOH, WOW! IT MELTED!!
?
OOOKAY.
ぐに
SQUEEZE
LET'S WORK IT!
ぐに
SQUEEZE

ジャ TA
DAH!! ン!!
WOW, YOU MADE A FIGURE OUT OF THE MELTED GLASS!
IS THAT ME?
OOOH!
IT'S A PRESENT TO COMMEMORATE OUR MEETING YUNA!
THANK YOU, PLEAKLEY! I'M SO HAPPY!
STITCH WANNA HOLD IT, TOO!
ACK!
SLIP
CRASH
ACK!
STIIIIIITCH!

SNIFF, SNIFF!

STITCH ENTERS THE COSTUME FESTIVAL!

Introducing Dr. Jumba and Pleakley,

who have come to Izayoi to find Stitch.

OOH, SO THIS IS STITCH'S AUNT AND UNCLE.

GAHA-HAHA!

NICE TO MEET YOU.

...

NO, THEY'RE NOT.

They have become good friends with Yuna. One day...

HEY, I HEARD THERE'S A COSTUME CONTEST AT THE UPCOMING FESTIVAL!

COSTUME CONTEST?

ROWLF

THE WINNING TEAM GETS A YEAR'S SUPPLY OF CANDY!

TEAMS CHOOSE A THEME!

THEN THEY SIGN UP.

WE'RE WITCHES! ♡

READ THIS WAY

CANDY!
YEAR'S SUPPLY!!
TWINKLE
キラ
TWINKLE
キラ
OOH, IT SOUNDS FUN. ♪
HMM.
WHY DON'T THE FOUR OF US ENTER AS A TEAM?
LET'S DO IT! LET'S DO IT!
ALL RIGHT, WE'RE NOW "TEAM YUNA"!
AND WHAT WILL THE COSTUME THEME BE FOR "TEAM YUNA"?
OH, RIGHT. HEY, I KNOW!

FANCY ANIMAL MASCOTS!
GORILLA.
RABBIT!
OSTRICH.
DOG.
Yuna's Vote
NO, ACTION!
BOOM! BWEEEM! EYAHAHA-HAHA!
Stitch's Vote

THIS IS THE EAST ASIAN ISLAND OF IZAYOI! THEREFORE, KABUKI THEATER MAKEUP!
Jumba's Vote
CONTESTS ARE WON BY BEING FLAM-BOYANT! LET'S MAKE THE CON-TEST INTO A DANCE PARTY!
Pleakley's Vote

...
FANCY IS BEST!
BAMBAM-BAM! BOOM! BOOOOOM!
EASTERN MYTHO-LOGICAL JAPANESE KABUKI THEATER!
DANCING, WITH A DISCO PLATFORM!
YOU LOOK WEIRD LIKE THAT!
WHY? IT'S FANCY!
YUNA, I WON'T BE A GORIL-LA.
BAMBA BAM! BO BOOOOO
EWW, NO WAY!
I'M AGAINST FIGHT-ING!
JAPANESE KABUKI THEATER IS THE BEST! KABUKI!
FANCY!!
SHOUT
YELL
On the day of the contest
AND THAT WAS "TEAM MON-STER"!
THANKS FOR COMING!
CLAP
CLAP
CLAP
NEXT IS "TEAM YUNA"!
COME ON OUT!

WHAP
ぶすぅ
WHAAAAAAA?
MURMUR
MURMUR
ざわ
LOOK!
AT THAT!
WHAA?

IF WE COULDN'T DECIDE ON A THEME, THEN WE SHOULD'VE JUST NOT COME AT ALL!!
NOT JOINING IS LIKE GIVING UP AND RUNNING AWAY BEFORE WE EVEN STARTED! WE CAN'T DO THAT!
ヒソ PSST!
ヒソ PSST!
LIKE I SAID, IF YOU JUST WORE MY DANCE COSTUMES...
ヒソ PSST!
NO WAY! THAT'S HORRIBLE.
TSK!
BOOM! BOOOOM!

YEEEEEAH!
AMAZING!
IT'S GREAT!
HUH?
WHAT?!

THAT WAS AN INTENSE DEBATE.
THE WINNER IS "TEAM YUNA"!
HUH, BUT WHY??
ワァー
YEEEEEEAH!
YOUR "ALIEN" COSTUMES! THEY WERE AMAZING!
A... ALIEN?!
THERE'S CERTAINLY SOMETHING APPEALING ABOUT AN EVIL SCIENTIST.
THAT'S RIGHT! ♪
CANDY! YAY! ♥
I'M JUST WEARING NORMAL CLOTHES!
I DON'T EVEN LOOK LIKE AN ALIEN!

STITCH DOES LAUNDRY!

THAT'S PROBABLY KODAMA.
KODAMA?
A TREE SPIRIT.
THERE ARE MANY YOKAI AND SPIRITS LIVING ON THE ISLAND.

THAT'S RIGHT. THERE ARE MANY MYSTERIOUS CREATURES ON THIS ISLAND!
LIFE FORMS NOT FOUND ON OTHER ISLANDS?
THIS ISLAND IS APPEALING FROM A RESEARCH STANDPOINT.
THAT'S RIGHT. YOU TWO HAVE NEVER SEEN THE "CHITAMA STONE."
THE "CHITAMA STONE"?

READ THIS WAY

YEP! IT'S A HUGE STONE DEEP IN THE FOREST.
THE STONE WILL GRANT ANY WISH.
ANY-THING?
HOHO... I AM DEEPLY INTEREST-ED IN THIS STONE.
STITCH WILL BE STRON-GEST IN THE UNIVERSE!
BUT IT WON'T GRANT YOUR WISH UNTIL YOU'VE DONE 43 "GOOD DEEDS."
43?
SO ALL YOU HAVE TO DO IS PERFORM 43 "GOOD DEEDS."
THAT'S STILL IMPOSSI-BLE FOR STITCH!
HMPH!
GAHAHAHA
ALL RIGHT! I'LL MAKE SOME-THING NICE FOR YOU BY TOMORROW, STITCH.

ジャーーーン!
TADAAAAH!
The next day...
...
I HAVE INVENTED THE "GOOD DEED COUNTER."
FOR EVERY GOOD DEED DONE, THE COUNTER GOES UP BY ONE.
SO THE COUNTER JUST NEEDS TO REACH 43, RIGHT?
HUH, IT ALREADY SAYS 01.
AH, THAT'S BECAUSE YOU CARRIED GRANDMA'S GROCERIES YESTERDAY!
OOOH! "GOOD DEED"!!
GRANDMA, I DO "GOOD DEED"! GRANDMA!
DASH
HE MAY BE SUPER INTELLI-GENT, BUT HE STILL CAN'T TELL THE DIFFERENCE BETWEEN RIGHT AND WRONG.
NOW I'M WOR-RIED!

READ THIS WAY

OH, WHAT IS IT, STITCH?
STITCH DO "GOOD DEED"!
OH, WILL YOU HELP ME?
WELL, HOW ABOUT YOU HELP ME DO THE LAUNDRY?
OK!!
HMM.
GRAB!
Washi
PUT IN DETERGENT.
Washi!
DUMP
POKE
SWITCH ON!
HMM?
NOT MOVING...

THIS ONE?
ズボッ
CLICK
BAM
HERE?
BADUM
しーん…
SILENCE
...
GRAAAAAGH
NOT. MOVING.
SHAKE
RATTLET
STITCH DO IT!!
DON DON

NEXT, GO OUTSIDE.
ドゴッ
SPLOP
WATER!!
ザーッ
SPRAY
ズル
SQUEAK
ズル
SQUEAK
びちゃ
SPLISH
びちゃ
SPLISH
せっせ
DRIP
せっせ
DRIP
DID "GOOD DEED"!
HEE HEE
ACK! WHAT ARE YOU DOING, STITCH?!
HM?
ザー

GYAH, MY FAVORITE DRESS IS POLKA DOT NOW.
DID YOU PUT IN A WHOLE BOX OF DETERGENT?
EMPTY
HEEY, THE COUNTER WENT BACK DOWN TO ZERO SINCE YOU BROKE THE WASHING MACHINE.
MMMRRR
GRANDMA!
THAT'S NOT TRUE! STITCH WAS BEING MY LITTLE HELPER.
THANK YOU, STITCH!
STITCH WASH AGAIN!
WE... WE'RE OKAY FOR TODAY.
GAHAHAHA!
I, THE EVIL SCIENTIST, DR. JUMBA, WILL HAVE THIS FIXED UP BRAND NEW IN NO TIME!

STITCH HELPS TARO!
Today, Yuna is taking Jumba and Pleakley out.
We're going to see the "Chitama Stone."
SO THIS IS THE FABLED "CHITAMA STONE."
WOOOOOW, HOW MYS-TICAL!
JUST HURRY UP AND DO YOUR 43 GOOD DEEDS.
THEN YOUR WISH WILL COME TRUE, STITCH! ♡
WHAT WAS STITCH'S WISH AGAIN?
STITCH WILL BE STRON-GEST IN THE UNIVERSE!
HEHE... TAKE A LOOK AT YOUR "GOOD DEED COUNTER," STITCH.
SMIRK

ジャーン!
TA
DAAAH
SO, YOU HAVEN'T BEEN DOING ANY GOOD DEEDS.
HMM!
HOW WEIRD... THE COUNTER STILL SEEMS TO BE AT 00.
THAT'S BECAUSE YOU LOSE THE POINTS YOU'VE ACCUMULATED IF YOU DO SOMETHING BAD. WATCH OUT!
THINK HE'LL BE ALL RIGHT?
WELL, HE'S ENTHUSIASTIC!
OOH! DO "GOOD DEED"!
びゅーん
DASH

READ
THIS
WAY

GOOD DEED... GOOD DEED.
キョロ GLANCE
キョロ GLANCE
WAAAAH! WHAT'LL I DO?
HM?
WHAT HAP-PEN?
OH, YOU YUNA'S FRIEND, RIGHT?
ME STITCH!
DO "GOOD DEED"!
I'M TARO.
I TRIPPED AND DROPPED MY TEXTBOOK INTO THE RIVER.
...
WHAT'LL I DO? IT GOT TAKEN DOWN-STREAM.
SHAAAAAH
HMM. STITCH STRONG, BUT HATE WATER!

WAS THAT YOUR STOMACH? I HAVE SOME LEFTOVERS FROM LUNCH THAT YOU CAN HAVE.
RICE BALL!
GURGLE
HMM... HMM.
THINKING MAKE ME HUNGRY!
AAH! NOT THE HANDKER-CHIEF, TOO!
THANK YOU!
が
SCARF
ば
WELL, THAT'S GOOD.
STOMACH ALL SETTLED!
HM? WHAT THIS?
ズルズルー
FPPT
FPPT
THE HANDKER-CHIEF'S ALL SLOBBERY.
ACK!
TARO, COME!
ぐいっ
YANK

READ THIS WAY

At Dr. Jumba's house…
DR. JUMBA, YUNA'S TEXTBOOK!
MATH
WHA?
AHH!
WHO ARE THESE PEOPLE?!
SO, YOUR TEXTBOOK FELL INTO THE RIVER?
YES, SIR.
HEE HEE. WELL, WE COULD GET IT BACK FOR YOU.
BUT I, THE EVIL SCIENTIST, DR. JUMBA, WILL MAKE YOU SOME-THING BETTER!
ガハハ～
GAHAHAHAHA
MATH
..
..
TADAH
ジャーン

SWITCH, ON!
PIII
CLANK
WAAAAH!
THE CONTENTS OF THE TEXT-BOOK ARE PRO-JECTED FROM ITS EYES AS A HOLOGRAM!
KANAKO
600 YEN
SHINJI
470 YEN
ALSO, IT WILL ORALLY EXPLAIN THE IMPORTANT POINTS TO YOU.
KANAKO BOUGHT ONE CAKE AND FOUR CREAM PUFFS AND PAID 680 YEN.
SHINJI BOUGHT ONE CAKE AND TWO CREAM PUFFS.
AND IT EVEN TAKES NOTES!
WOOOOW, AMAZING, JUMBA!
I CAN'T BRING THIS TO SCHOOL!
MOM'S GOING TO YELL AT ME!
OOOH!
TARO!
HM?

READ THIS WAY
THERE YOU ARE, TARO.
YUNA!
YOUR MOM'S WORRIED SICK ABOUT YOU BEING OUT SO LATE.
BUT, MY TEXT-BOOK!
HUH?

IT WAS AN ACCI-DENT. JUST TELL YOUR MOM, AND SHE'LL UN-DERSTAND.
IT'S NOT LIKE SHE'LL GET MAD AT YOU.
BUT-!
TARO GOOD KID!
GAVE STITCH RICE BALL! WE GO HOME TOGETHER!
STITCH!
EWW, IT'S COVERED IN SPIT.

THE GOOD DEED COUNTER IS BACK UP TO 01.
STITCH DOES HAVE A GOOD SIDE TO HIM, HUH?
BYE BYE, TARO!
BYE, YUNA!
THANKS!
カ BEEP
チッ CLICK
The next morning...
UNFORTUNATELY, I ALREADY PUT YOUR TEXTBOOK INTO THIS ROBOT.
SINCE I CAN'T GET IT BACK OUT, YOU'LL NEED TO STUDY WITH THIS, YUNA.
GAHAHA
I CAN'T BRING THIS TO SCHOOL!
Shortly thereafter, Taro got his textbook from the river.
GREAT!
MATH

READ
THIS
WAY

Pleakley, the leading Earth expert (or so he claims)…
COSPLAY FAN
Dr. Jumba, the evil scientist and Stitch's creator…
YUNA FORGETS HER HOMEWORK!
SO, JUMBA AND PLEAKLEY, YOU'RE STITCH'S OHANA?
HMM, SOMETHING LIKE THAT.
TEEHEE
…
These two aliens also came to Izayoi.
They've become good friends with Yuna.
Then, one evening…
OH NO, I FORGOT MY HOMEWORK!

オロ SOB
オロ SOB
WHAT'LL I DO? I NEED TO HAND IT IN TOMORROW!
WHAT IS THIS "HOMEWORK"?
I BELIEVE IT'S SOME SORT OF WORK GIVEN OUT AT THAT "SCHOOL" THING.
WHAT HOMEWORK WAS IT?
ART HOMEWORK WHERE I MAKE "ME GROWN UP" OUT OF CLAY.
ART? I'M GREAT AT THAT!♪ NEED HELP?
OH, REALLY?
YUNA!
ギロッ GLARE
YOU MUST DO YOUR HOMEWORK ON YOUR OWN!
YES, GRANDMA.
AAAH, IS IT ALREADY SEVEN O'CLOCK?
I NEED TO HURRY AND GET THIS DONE!
SQUEEZE こねっ
SQUEEZE こねっ
SQUEEZE こねっ
UGH!
...

READ THIS WAY
SHOCK
YUNA, MAYBE YOU'RE JUST BAD AT CRAFTS?
NN... NOT AT ALL!
RUSTLE
RUSTLE
OH! LOOK!
HM?
AGH, STITCH!
WHAT'S THIS?
THIS IS CLAY.
TADA!
SNICKER
YOU'RE REALLY BAD AT THIS!
I...I MADE THIS WHEN I WAS A LOT YOUNGER!
THE DATE IS SPRING... OF THIS YEAR.
HEE
HEE
IT'S TITLED "ME."
OKAY, I'M BAD AT CRAFTS!
I'M AWFUL AT IT AND I DON'T KNOW WHAT TO MAKE!

THE THEME IS "ME GROWN UP," RIGHT?
SO IT'S AS SIMPLE AS MAKING IT IN THE IMAGE OF WHAT YOU WANT TO BE IN THE FUTURE!
I HAVE SOMETHING I WANT TO BE, BUT I'M NO GOOD AT PUTTING IT INTO A SHAPE.
NNG... UGG.
GAH, IT'S NO GOOD.
GYA-HA-HA-HA!
PLOP
CHUCK
SHE REALLY IS AWFUL ...
HA HA, NOW IT'S MY TURN.
I, THE EVIL SCIENTIST, DR. JUMBA, WILL UNVEIL MY GREAT INVENTION!
IT'S THE "DESIGNER PATCH"!

SLAP
JUST PUT THIS ON YOUR FOREHEAD.
AND THEN?
BWAAAAA!
H... HEY!
THE MACHINE STIMULATES THE CREATIVITY CENTER IN YOUR BRAIN THROUGH YOUR FOREHEAD.
AND THEN YOU BECOME MORE CREATIVE!
THIS IS AMAZING!
I CAN IMAGINE IT NOW.
FWOOOOO
WOW!
AMAZING!
OOOH!

I'LL HOLD AND INTER-NATIONAL EXHIBITION FOR CHITAMA-STYLE KARATE!
I'LL COMPETE IN THE OLYMPICS!
I'LL BE A CHARISMATIC COMPANY PRESIDENT!
バ BDA
バ BDA
バ BDA
バ BDA
バ BDA
バ BDA
バ BDA
A FLIGHT ATTEN-DANT!
A SUPER-MODEL!
A PRE-SCHOOL TEACHER!
I CAN MAKE ANYTHING ...!
1
YUNA SURE HAS A LOT OF DREAMS, HUH?
STITCH HAS DREAM!
NO CONSISTENCY IN HER DREAMS. CHILDLIKE FANTA-SIES ARE QUITE WONDERFUL.
GAHAHA!
STITCH WILL BE STRONGEST IN THE UNIVERSE!

READ THIS WAY

HAAAAH
FINISHED ...

THAT'S GREAT, YUNA! YOU MADE SO MANY.
TEEHEE, THANKS! ♡
YAAAWN!
I'M REALLY EXHAUSTED.
YAAAAAAWN

YAAAAWN
THAT'S BECAUSE YOUR BRAIN WAS OVER-STIM-ULATED AND YOU WORKED SO HARD.
YOU NEED TO GET YOUR REST.
SLEEP TIGHT, YUNA.
GOOD NIIIIIGHT!

The next day...
OH NO!
バタ
BUM
I SLEPT IN AND NOW I'M GONNA BE LATE!
BE SAFE!
バタ
BUM
バタ
BUM
ムクッ
GRCK
AAAAWN
HM?

AFTER I WORKED SO HARD...
I FORGOT TO BRING MY PROJECT!
ガーン
OH
NO

STITCH MEETS KIJIMUNAA!
Today, Yuna and Stitch have come to the forest in search of Kijimunaa, the most powerful of the yokai.
I WONDER WHAT HE'S LIKE.
STITCH WANNA SEE WHO STRONGEST!

However...
GAAH, WE'VE LOOKED EVERYWHERE!
KIJIMUNAA, WHERE ARE YOU?
STITCH HUNGRY!
CHEW
CHEW
AAAGH! STOP IT! YOU'LL HURT THE TREE!

WELL, IT'S NOON, SO LET'S EAT LUNCH.
YANK!
RICE BALLS.
AND THESE ARE THE SIDE DISHES.
MMM
YUM
ぬう
GROOUUUN
POP!
PLUNK
PLUNK
HUH?
SOME RICE BALLS ARE MISSING.

READ THIS WAY
STITCH! I'M ALWAYS TELL-ING YOU, YOU CAN'T EAT UNTIL YOU SAY GRACE!
STITCH DIDN'T EAT! YUNA TOOK IT!
I DIDN'T EAT IT!
STITCH NO EAT IT EITHER!
GROOOUN
GRR!
GRR!
HUH?
EEEK!
PTEW!
SOMEONE CAME OUT OF THE TREE!
スポ
POP!

SHFT
SHFT
SHFT
WHAT'S THAT? HEY, IT'S GETTING AWAY!
STRANGE GUY!
I WONDER, MAYBE THAT KID'S KIJIMUNAA.
OOH!
WAIT, KIJIMUNAA!
DASH
ACK!
POP
POP
POP

READ THIS WAY

A... AMAZING! HE HAS THE POWER TO HIDE INSIDE TREES.
HAH
HAH
CAN'T CATCH HIM!
TWITCH
TWITCH
ALL RIGHT, WE NEED A PLAN.
PSST
PSST
HAAAH, OH WELL. LET'S GIVE UP FOR TODAY AND HEAD HOME, STITCH.
OKAY, YUNA.
...
HEY!
STITCH, WHAT'S WRONG?
THERE'S A GIANT MUSHROOM GROWING OUT OF YOUR HEAD!
OOH! THAT'S RIGHT!
WHY'S THAT?? HMM... AMAAAAAAAZ-ING!

POKE
GRAWRGH
ドバーン
BAAAAAAAAAM
PWAAAAAAAA
ドゴッ
BADUM
ド
DOM
サッ
SHFT
SO YOU'RE KIJIMUNAA ...

I... I'M KIJIMUNAA.
I WAS HUNGRY AND... I'M SORRY.
DON'T WORRY 'BOUT IT!
BY THE WAY, I'M YUNA.
STITCH!
I... DON'T HAVE ANY FRIENDS... SO IF YOU'D BE MY FRIENDS...
STITCH BE YOUR FRIEND!
FFT
YEP, ICHARIBA CHOODEE, RIGHT!
CLICK
BEEP
NICE TO MEETCHA, KIJIMUNAA! ♡

STITCH IS A SUPER STAR SKATER?!
IT'S ALWAYS HOT HERE ON THIS TROPICAL ISLAND, EVEN NOW IN THE WINTER.
IT'D BE FUN TO HAVE IT SNOW.
YEAH, WE COULD HAVE A SNOWBALL FIGHT, OR GO SLEDDING AND SKIING.
AAH, RIGHT! JUMBA, COULD YOU MAKE A MACHINE LIKE THAT? A SNOW MACHINE!
HOHO, OF COURSE! IT'S QUITE SIMPLE.
GAHAHA
YUNA!
HUH?!

READ THIS WAY
IT WOULD BE QUITE A SHOCK TO ALL THE TREES AND ANIMALS IF IT WERE TO SNOW HERE, ON A TROPICAL ISLAND!
IT WOULD BE WRONG TO GO AGAINST MOTHER NATURE!
OKAAAY.
HMM... BUT MY IN-TELLECTUAL GENIUS...
じゃーーん☆
TADAH!
JUST PERFECT FOR SKATING, NO?
YOU TURNED THE SCHOOL POOL INTO A SKATING RINK!
Figure-skating costumes, courtesy of Pleakley...
WOW!
AMAZ-ING!
Piko
Kouji
Siblings going to Yuna's elementary school...

SSSSSSSSSKT
WHEE! THIS IS SO MUCH FUN!
YUNA'S SO GREAT AT ICE SKATING, EVEN FOR HER FIRST TIME!
YUNA, THAT OUT-FIT LOOKS DIVINE ON YOU. ♡
SSSSSSKT
スイー
PIKO, YOU OKAY?
SLAM
AAAACK!
HOW COME YUNA CAN SKATE SO WELL? IT'S HER FIRST TIME ON THE ICE!
DO SOMETHING ABOUT IT, KOUJI!
HEE HEE, LEAVE IT TO ME.
Not moving since he can't skate...

KICK
SHAAAAAAAA
BAAAAAA
AAAAAAAAAA!
DOM
THAT KID TRIPPED HER ON PURPOSE!
AHAHAHA-HAHA!
HEY, YUNA, YOUR UN-DERWEAR IS SHOWING!

ダッ
DASH
YUNA!
OW OW OW!
IT'S OKAY, STITCH.
I LOOKED KINDA DUMB, HUH?
YOU SHOULDN'T WORRY ABOUT IT. THE ONE GOOD THING ABOUT YUNA IS THAT SHE'S DURABLE!
GRRR-ROWL
ぐいっ
GRAB
WHAA?!
ぐるん
SPIN
ぐるん
SPIN
ぐるん
SPIN
ぐるん
SPIN
WHAA?!
WHAA?!

LOOK! THAT'S AMAZING!
AAAAAGGH!!
ガバァ
GURAH!
シャアア…ーーッ
SSSSSSSKT
WHOOOA!
WOW!
IT'S A FIGURE SKATING LIFT!
シャアアア
SSSSSSSKT

TOSS
SPIN!
クル
TWIRL
クル
TWIRL
クル
TWIRL
クル
TWIRL
WHOOOOA!
POSE
TADAH!

READ THIS WAY
ワァァァァ
WOOOOOOW!
YOU'RE AMAZING, STITCH!
パチ CLAP
パチ CLAP
パチ CLAP
パチ CLAP
N... NO WAY! I WON'T FORGET THIS!
くらくら～ DIZZY
PLAH
BADUM
THANKS, STITCH!
HE HE!

ECIAL EDITION
LILO AND STITCH
♬A STORY ABOUT STITCH'S EXCITING ADVENTURES IN HAWAII♪
LILO
A five-year-old girl living on the island of Kauai in Hawaii. She lived alone with her sister Nani after losing her parents to an accident, but after meeting Stitch, they now live together as ohana (family).
NANI
Lilo's sister. She raises Lilo in place of their parents. Stitch is always causing her trouble with his mischievous ways.
A self-proclaimed leading Earth expert, he is gathering information for the Galactic Council. He came together with Dr. Jumba to look for Stitch, but now lives together on Hawaii with Lilo and her friends.
PLEAKELY
DAVID
ani's boyfriend. 's understanding about how busy Nani is.
DR. JUMBA
A self-proclaimed evil scientist and Stitch's creator. He came to Earth to capture Stitch, but is currently living with Lilo.

STITCH MAKES A CAKE
Lilo and the alien Stitch are ohana living together in Hawaii.
"Ohana" is a Hawaiian word meaning "family."
HEY STITCH, WHAT ARE YOU LOOKIN' AT?
A CAKE BOOK?
The two of them live together with Nani, Lilo's sister.
CAKE?
THE CAKE BOOK
Cake
Today is Ohana Day, a day once a month where they spend time together as a family.
NANI
THAT THING MY SISTER'S ALWAYS MAKING.
NANI'S CAKE
CAKE IN THE BOOK
BUT SHE'S REALLY BAD AT COOKING...
OH, THAT'S RIGHT! TODAY'S OHANA DAY!
LET'S SURPRISE NANI AND MAKE HER A CAKE! IT'LL BE OUR SECRET.
おーっ
Cake
OH, AMAZING! YOU MADE THIS, LILO?
EHEHE

WHAT ARE YOU MAK-ING? CAKE SOUNDS GOOD TO ME!
OH, CAKE? YOU CAN JUST LEAVE THAT TO ME!
Dr. Jumba, an evil scientist and Stitch's creator
Pleakley, an alien and Earth fan
READY? GO GET THE THINGS I'M ABOUT TO READ OUT TO YOU, STITCH. ♡
OK!
FIRST, SOME "EGG" THINGS THAT COME FROM THE FEMALE EARTH-BIRDS CALLED "CHICKENS!"
CLUCK
CLUCK
CLUCK
AND SOME OF THAT CALCIUM DRINK "MILK" THAT COMES FROM FEMALE COWS.
MOOO
SQUIRT
SQUIRT

READ THIS WAY
NEXT, THAT PROCESSED "BUTTER" AND "CREAM."
BUTTER
CREAM
SODIUM CRYS-TALLINE "SUGAR."
AND A TYPE OF DUST MADE FROM WHEAT CALLED "WHEAT FLOUR."
WHEAT FLOUR
SUGAR
"FRUITS" BORN FROM THE FLOWERS OF VEGETA-TION!
AAAND...
... ...
ALL RIGHT, WE GOT THE INGREDI-ENTS.
LET'S BAKE! ♡
THANKS, STITCH! ♡
EHEHE

SO, I WANNA MAKE A CAKE LIKE THIS!
HMM, A PORTRAIT CAKE.
OKAY! WELL, I'LL MAKE A MACHINE THEN.
ガチャ SHUFFLE
WITH A PUSH OF A BUTTON, IT WILL MAKE THE SPONGE CAKE AND ICING!
ガチャ SHUFFLE
...

YOU REALLY NEED TO PUT YOUR HEART INTO MAKING THIS CAKE!
STIR STIR STIR STIR
YOU NEED TO MAKE THE SPONGE CAKE AND ICING BY HAND!
HMM ...
HOW PRIMI-TIVE!
STIR STIR
STITCH, TAKE THIS SERIOUSLY!
JUMBA, MY ARMS HUUU-UURT.
TOUGH IT OUT!
SHAKE
SHAKE
WE DID IT!
THUD

READ THIS WAY

IT WAS SUPPOSED TO BE A PORTRAIT CAKE.
BUT WE WANTED IT TO BE EVEN BETTER, SO WE MADE THE WHOLE BODIES! GREAT, HUH? ♡
MY CAKE BASE AND DECORATIVE SPACESHIP ARE PRETTY AMAZING, RIGHT?
IT ACTUALLY FLIES!
SPACESHIP!
RIDE!
BOUND
BOUND
THUD
HEY, STOP!
BOUND
BOUND
SCREEEEEECH
DON'T STAND ON THE BASE.
IT'LL COL-LAPSE!

どごーーーん
SCREEE-CRASH
OH NO!
ぐちゃーーー
SPLAT
RUINED!
AAAH
ちらっ
SNIFFLE
ガーーーン
SHOCK
UUUUU-WAAAAA-AAGH!
STITCH, I HATE YOU!

SIIGH
WHAT SHOULD WE DO?
I DON'T KNOW.
WHAT IS THIS MESS?!
OH, NANI, WELCOME BACK.
LET'S SEE.
LILO, I FINISHED PREPARA-TIONS FOR OHANA DAY.
POP
COME ON DOWN, PLEASE.
DON'T WANNA!
NOPE, WE PROMISED TO SPEND OHANA DAY TOGETHER WITH EVERY-ONE, DIDN'T WE?
YANK
BUT...!
JUST COME ON.

ジャーーン!
TA-DA!
LILO
リロ
LOVE
THE CAKE IS BACK TO-GETHER!
STITCH WORKED REALLY HARD TO FIX IT.
BUT IT STILL LOOKS A LITTLE ROUGH.
SORRY, LILO.
NO, STITCH, I'M THE ONE WHO'S SORRY!
Lilo and Stitch managed to make up.
IT'S PRETTY CUTE IF YOU LOOK AT IT CLOSELY. ♡
IT IS! ♡
WELL, LET'S EAT! ♡
It turned out to be a great Ohana Day!
YUCK, DISGUST-ING.
JUDGING BY THE TASTE, YOU CAN TELL THEY'RE SISTERS ...

EHYAHYA!

FIND THE MYSTERIOUS BUTTERFLY!

READ
THIS
WAY

THIS MACHINE I MADE HAS THE DATA ON ALL SORTS OF BUTTERFLIES.
IF THAT RARE BUTTERFLY COMES WITHIN A 100-MILE RADIUS, AN ALARM WILL SOUND AND LET US KNOW ITS LOCATION.
AMAZING, ISN'T IT?
ピコーン WHOOP
ピコーン WHOOP
OH, THE ALARM! LET'S LOOK TEN METERS TO THE SOUTH.
YES SIR!
MR. RARE BUTTERFLY!
COME OUT HERE!
キョロ GLANCE
キョロ GLANCE
PRICKLE
FLUTTER FLUTTER
OOH!
GRAAAAAANCH
BUTTERFLY!

AACK!
バキ
CRUNCH
バキ
CRUNCH
OOOW!
ドカァ!!
BRUMPF
AGH, IT GOT AWAY!
STITCH!
THAT'S DANGER-OUS, STITCH!
?
WHOOP
WHOOP
OH, IT CAME BACK!
LET'S LOOK, EVERY-ONE!
MR. BUTTER-FLY...
キョロ
GLANCE
キョロ
GLANCE
THIS TIME TO THE WEST!
YEP
BZZZZZZZZZ
BZZZ
BZZZ
HM?

READ THIS WAY

SNAP
?
ブン BUZZ
?
BUZZ ブン
AAAAAACK!
OW
ブン BUZZ
OW
IT HURTS, IT HURTS!
?
ガジ MUNCH
ガジ MUNCH
BUUUUUUUU ブーン
BUZZ ブン
BUZZ ブン

HA-RUMPH. STITCH, YOU DOLT!
THIS IS HORRIBLE!
SPIT
SPIT
ボコ STING
ボコ STING
ビー BEEEEEEEP
WHAT'S THAT?
ビー BEEEEEEEP
ビー BEEEEEEEP

POKE
THIS IS THE ALARM FOR BUTTERFLIES THAT AREN'T IN THE SYSTEM.
NO WAY...A NEW TYPE?
THIS IS AMAZING! WHERE, JUMBA, WHERE??
BEEP
BEEP
BEEP
BEEP
AAACK!
GAHA
HUH, WHAT IS IT?
HA!
I SEE.
HIS EARS ARE ABLE TO SENSE SUPERSONIC WAVES AS WELL.
HE MUST BE HEARING THE FLAPPING OF THE BUTTER-FLY'S WINGS AND HEADING THERE!
THEN LET'S CHASE AF-TER HIM! HURRY!
TWFFT
TWFFT
TWFFT
TWFFT
TWFFT
WHOA!
TWFFT

TWFFT
THERE THEY ARE! THEY'RE SO PRETTY... ♡
IT REALLY IS A NEW TYPE. AMAZING!
WELL, LET'S CATCH IT! ♡
WE'LL RAISE IT SECRETLY, SO NANI DOESN'T KNOW. ♡
WHAT ARE YOU TALKING ABOUT? IF WE CATCH IT AND GIVE IT TO A BUTTERFLY COLLECTOR, THEY'LL DEFINITELY GIVE US A REWARD!
CO... COLLECTOR?
THAT'S RIGHT! IT'LL PROBABLY BE MADE INTO A SPECIMEN AND SHOWN OFF AT A MUSEUM.
THE FIND OF THE CENTURY!
GAHAHA
WAIT.

NO!
THAT'S AWFUL!
ピクン
TWITCH
ぱっ
JUMP!
バキ
SNAP
EGYAH! WHAT ARE YOU DOING? MY NET!
ガバ
GRAGH
バキ
SNAP
ビリビリ
CHEW
CHEW
ドゴン
KTHUNK
NO, STOP! NOT THE MACHINE!
STITCH!
HRMPH!

ふわっ
FLIT
FLUTTER
パタ
FLUTTER
パタ
AAAHN
FLUTTER
パタ
BYE BYE, MR. BUTTERFLY. ♡
THE DISCOVERY OF THE CENTURY!
AWWW!
THE MACHINE YOU DESTROYED HAD THE NAVIGATIONAL FUNCTIONALITY BUILT IN IT.
ホー
HOOT
ホー
HOOT
...
WHERE ARE WE? WE'RE LOST! WE'LL NEVER GET HOME!

STITCH IS A TALENTED ARTIST?!
LOOK, STITCH.
THERE'S A "CHILDREN'S ART EXHIBIT" COMING UP!
EX-HIB-IT?
CHILDREN'S ART EXHIBIT
IT'S WHERE YOU DRAW A PICTURE AND THEN THEY DISPLAY IT AT THE TOWN MUSEUM.
THE THEME IS "CUTE ANI-MALS"!!
OF COURSE I'LL DRAW YOU, STITCH!
OOH!
HEE HEE!
SO YOU'LL ENTER, TOO?
MERTLE!

フフン!
SNORT
WHAT ARE YOU GOING TO DRAW, LILO?
I'M GOING TO DRAW MY ADORABLE LITTLE PET DOGGY.
STITCH!
GIGI
THE THEME IS "CUTE," YOU KNOW!
THERE'S NOTHING CUTE ABOUT THAT DOG OF YOURS!!
TWITCH
STITCH IS TOO CUTE!
WHAT PART? THAT FE-ROCIOUS MUTT ...
ボカ
KICK
ビリビリ
ビリ
RRRAGGGH
TUSTLE
スカ
THERE'S ABSOLUTELY NO WAY I'M GONNA LOSE TO YOU!
ベー!
BLEEEEEH
いー!
BLAAAAH
FUNNY, THAT'S WHAT I WANTED TO SAY. I WON'T LOSE!

OKAY, STITCH.
JUST SIT STILL.
...
DON'T MOVE, OKAY?
YOU'RE A MODEL.
FFT FFT FFT
RIGHT. LOOK-ING GOOD.
FFT FFT FFT FFT
TWITCH TWITCH
WRIGGLE
TWITCH TWITCH
BA
BA BA BA
GRAA WRG
CHEW CHEW CHEW
DON'T MOVE, STITCH!
POSE
STITCH!
POSE

ゆら
TWITCH
...
TWITCH
ゆら
うずうず うず うずうず
WRIGGLE
WRIGGLE
SPLASH
バシャ
SPLASH
バシャ
STIIIIIITCH!
LILO, COULD YOU COME HERE FOR A SEC?
IT'S NANI. YOU WAIT HERE AND BE GOOD, OKAY, STITCH?
...
DON'T MOVE!
ばっ
BADUM
CLUNK*

?
ぶちゅう〜〜
BLOOSH
BLOOSH
ぶちゅ
OOOH!
ぶちゅ
OOSH
ぶちゅ
BLOOSH
PICTURE
絵っ
PICTURE
絵っ
SCHLP
SCHLP
SCHLP
RIIIIP
バリ
バリー
RIIIIP
SCHLP
絵ーっ♪
PICTURE

READ THIS WAY
OH NO!
IT'S RUINED!
AAAH!
MMRRRR
ポイッ TOSS
MERTLE WILL MAKE FUN OF ME FOR THIS.
HMPH, I GIVE UP. YOU RUINED IT, STITCH!
AAAH, FIGHTING AGAIN?
WELL!
STITCH NEVER TAKES ANYTHING SERIOUSLY!
OH, IS THIS WHAT STITCH MADE?
HMM... HOW ORIGINAL.
ぷw SNIFFLE
ぷw SNIFFLE
THERE, THERE.
SINCE IT'S ALREADY DONE, WHY DON'T WE ENTER IT? IN STITCH'S NAME!
THIS?

That week-end...
WOW!
AMAZING!
SHOCK
THIS PAINTING IS A WORK OF ART THAT WILL GO DOWN IN HISTORY!
THIS IS THE SPECIAL JUDGE FOR THE EXHIBITION. HE'S AN INCREDIBLY FAMOUS ARTIST, YOU KNOW.
I DON'T GET IT.
RIGHT?
WOOOW, STITCH!
YOU PAINTED THIS?
?
AMAZING!
GRRRRAW!

SO, THIS IS HOW YOU MAKE IT ART?! ALL RIGHT!
SPLAT
SPLAT
SPLAT

LET'S TAKE A BATH!
YOU NEED TO TAKE A BATH, STITCH!
DON'T WANNA!
HE REALLY HATES WATER SINCE HIS BODY'S SO HEAVY. HE FLOATS LIKE A BRICK IN IT.
THERE'S NOT EVEN ENOUGH WATER IN THE TUB TO SINK!
THAT'S RIGHT. BATHS FEEL GREAT, STITCH. ♡
LET'S TAKE IT TOGETHER. ♪
BLECH
NO WAY!

STITCH!
ズル DRAG
ズル DRAG
GET IN THE BATH!
THERE'S BATH.
NEED TO TAKE BATH.
BATH BROKEN!
DON'T NEED TO TAKE BATH.
DESTROY!
GARUAH!
ACK!
SPLOOOOSH
CLANG
EEEK!

READ
THIS
WAY

STIIIIITCH!
THAT'S DANGER-OUS!
ぐいっ
SQUEEZE
ぐに
TWIST
ぐに
TWIST
ぐに
TWIST
ぐるん
SPIN
ぐるん
SPIN
AAAH! HELP MEEEE!
CUT IT OUT, STITCH!
ビュッ
BLOOSH
ビュッ
BLOOSH
SHAMPOO
ビュッ
BLOOSH

GRRAARWGH
CLANG
CLANG
CLANG
* TO ALL YOU GOOD CHILDREN, DON'T TRY THIS AT HOME!
YOU'RE BEING NAUGHTY, STITCH!
CLINK
HAH
HAH
STITCH... OHANA ARE TOGETHER FOREVER.
SO WE'RE GOING TO TAKE A BATH NOW. TOGETHER.
OHANA
TOGETHER FOREVER
LET'S GET IN!

ぴちょ
FAAAAAAAAAAH
ん…
LET'S MAKE SOME BUBBLES IN THE BATH.
PUT SOME BODY SOAP INTO THE WARM WATER.
シュコ
SHFT
シュコ
SHFT
BUBBLE?
HEY, IT'S PRETTY NICE IN THE BATH, ISN'T IT?
UH-HUH.
YAY!
ぷう
FFFFT
OOOH!
BUBBLE!
キラ
TWINKLE
キラ
TWINKLE

...
パッ
GRAB
BODY SOAP
ドポポポポ
BLUGLUGLUG
BODY SOAP
STITCH! NO, DON'T PUT IT ALL IN!
バババババーーッ
SPLASHASHASH
YAAA! THIS IS GREAT!
I LOVE BUBBLE BATHS!
ブク
BLUB
ブク
BLUB
ブク
BLUB
ブク
BLUB

READ THIS WAY
KA-CHA!
HEY, WHAT'RE YOU TWO DOING?
YOU'RE WASTING ALL THE BODY SOAP!
NANI!
SORRY!
IT'S CALLED A BUBBLE BATH.
THAT SOUNDS NICE.
HUH?
IT'S NICE TO DO SOMETHING LIKE THIS ONCE IN A WHILE!
HA. YOU'RE SO SILLY, STITCH!
WIGGLE WIGGLE ♥

WHERE
THIS?

HAPPINESS FROM THE SNOW MACHINE?!

THIS IS A HEATING INSTRUMENT USED IN JAPAN.
ドン
BANG
IT'S A SIMPLE CON-TRAPTION, BUT IT'S QUITE IMPRESSIVE.
AND A HOT POT!
PUT THE INGREDIENTS IN HERE, SIMMER, AND THEN EAT!
ジャーン
TADAAAAAH!
ぐつぐつ
BUBBLE
ぐつぐつ
BUBBLE
ぐつぐつぐつぐつ ぐつぐつぐつ
BUBBLE
HAAH
HAAH
HAAH
HAAH
...
I CAN'T TAKE IT!
バターン
THUD

ジャーン
TA-DA!
OF COURSE, THE BEST THING TO DO WHEN IT'S HOT IS TO HAVE SOMETHING COLD!
I DECIDED TO FREEZE OUR LUNCH.
FRIED CHICKEN
パリ
TWINKLE
SANDWICH
パリ
TWINKLE
CORN SOUP SHERBET
TWINKLE
パリ
A NICE, COOLING LUNCH!
SALAD
HAMBURGER STEAK
...
あっけ
AGAPE
IT FEELS GOOD TO THE TOUCH, AT LEAST.
ひんやり
FWAAAAAH
A ROCK-HARD STEAK IS TERRIBLE!
YUCK!
シャリ
CRUNCH
シャリ
CRUNCH
OH, HUH.
ガジ
CHEW
ガジ
CHEW
HARUMPH. IT WOULD BE BEST TO JUST DO THINGS LIKE NORMAL.
NORMAL?

PUT THE CHILLY-CHILLY ICE IN.
ガコッ KCHINK
ヴィ… VRRRRM ン
シャカ SHAKT
THEN MAKE SHAVED ICE WITH A SHAVED ICE MACHINE! ♡
SHAKT シャカ
SHAKT シャカ
ひんやり～～♡ FWAAAH
AAAH, THIS IS THE LIFE.
I'VE COME BACK FROM THE BRINK.
DEFI-NITELY!
RIGHT? NORMAL IS BEST! JUST NORMAL.
OOH!
キラキラキラ TWINKLE TWINKLE
PUT IN ICE.
SHAVED ICE!
SO!
YOU TAKE ICE.
ADD A FROZEN SAND-WICH
THEN MIX.
IT'S A SHAVED SAND-WICH!
わく DROOL
わく DROOL
わく DROOL
バッ GRAB

TOSS
ポイ
?!
CRUNCH
ジャリ
CRUNCH
ジャリ
BRRAAAA
バリ
ポイ
TOSS
CLANK
GATTA
ガガガガガ
GATTA
BRRAAAA
バリ
BA
HISS
プス
HISS
プス
BOOM
HUH?
STIIITCH!
IT BROKE!!

THERE'S NOTHING WE CAN DO NOW THAT IT'S BROKEN.
BUT STILL, I FEEL LIKE I'M GETTING HOT-TER AND HOT-TER. IT MUST BE FROM THE EXHAUSTION.
HAAH
BLAAAAAH
SIZZLE
SIZZLE
IF IT'D JUST SNOW LIKE IN THAT BOOK, I BET IT'D BE COOLER.
A SNOWY CHRISTMAS♥
DING!
DUN
DUN
DUN
DUN
BRRABABA
BRRA BABA
STITCH!
VREEEE
GATTA
GATTA
BADADADAAAAAH!
??

LILO! PRESS HERE.
HUH, PRESS THIS BUTTON?
BEEP
GRUH
GRUH
ヴィー
VROOOOOM
WOOOO
ゴォォ
GRAUH
AAAH! WHAT'S THAT?
OOOH!♡
IT'S SNOW!
HUH?
THIS IS SNOW?
STITCH MADE A SNOW MACHINE!
GA-HA-HA

SO, THIS IS SNOW.
OH, IT'S SO NICE!
THANK YOU, STITCH!
EHE.
DONE!
HUH, IS THAT ME?!
CRUNCH
CRUNCH
AHA, SO MUCH FUN!
CRUNCH
A...A... AH-CHOO!
SHIVER
SHIVER
IT'S GOTTEN CHILLY. THAT'S ENOUGH SNOW.
HUH? NOT STOPPING?
BEEP
BEEP
VREEEEEN
SHIVER
SHIVER
NO WAY, IT'S BROKEN!

DINNER, EVERYONE!
COOOOOOOMING! ♡
OPERATION: NANI'S DATE!
WHAT'S THIS?!
SIIIGH
ぽけ〜♡
IT'S A MESS!
THIS IS LUNCH?
IT'S JUST AN APPLE!
YOU SEE, DAVID INVITED NANI OUT ON AN AMAZING DATE.
THAT'S RIGHT. WE'RE GOING ON A LUXURY CRUISE SHIP.
WE'LL WATCH THE SUNSET FROM THE DECK.
THEN WE'LL HAVE DINNER THAT NIGHT AT A FANCY RESTAU-RANT. ♡

OH, YEAH! OH, YEAH!
WHY IS SHE SO EXCITED ABOUT THAT?
SHE'S SO EXCITED FOR IT THAT SHE HASN'T DONE ANY HOUSE-WORK.
WHY DID DAVID INVITE HER ON SUCH A FANCY DATE?
WELL, HE MUST'VE MADE HER MAD, RIGHT?
I'M SORRY, NANI!
HMPH
SO IT'S A DATE *AND* AN APOLOGY!
GAHAHA

ガシャーン
CRASH
EYAGH! I CAN'T BELIEVE IT!
ぐちゃ
SHATTER
ぐちゃ...
SHATTER
KNOWING MY SISTER, IF THE DATE DOESN'T GO WELL, WATCH OUT!
LISTEN, EVERYONE! I WANT YOU TO HELP MAKE NANI'S DATE GO OVER WELL!
BUT WHY?

TH...THAT'S RIGHT. I CAN'T LIVE IN THIS FILTHY PLACE ANY LONGER.
RIGHT! I'M TIRED OF THIS FOOD, TOO!
LET'S STRATEGIZE FOR A SUCCESS-FUL DATE!
RIGHT!

Operation 1
LOOK, NANI!
A FANCY DRESS!
IT'S FOR YOUR FANCY DATE!
I MADE IT MYSELF!
ICK!
OOH!
TWINKLE
TWINKLE
TWINKLE
TWINKLE
OOH!
LIGHT UP!
FUUUUN!
ACK! IS THAT MY BEST DRESS?! I WAS GOING TO WEAR THAT ON THE DATE!
SWISH
SWISH
WHY DID YOU ATTACH THESE LIGHT-BULBS TO IT?
GIVE IT BACK, STITCH!
NO!
WAIT!
TUG
RIIIIIP
AAAAAAAAAAAAAH!

SHAKE
Operation 2
WHEN NANI GETS UPSET, HER SKIN BREAKS OUT.
YOUR TURN, STITCH!
WAGGLE
OK!
GAAAH!
WHAT?
WHAT ARE YOU DOING, STITCH?
WAGGLE
WAGGLE
Hates bugs
SWING
SWING
STOP! STAY BACK!
WAGGLE
WAGGLE
AAAAAH!
NO, GET AWAY! AAAH! AAAH!
WITH JUST THE RIGHT AMOUNT OF EXERCISE, YOUR SKIN WILL BE BABY SMOOTH! GO FOR IT!

READ THIS WAY
Operation 3
IF YOU WANT YOUR DATE TO BE A SUCCESS, IT'S ALL IN THE HAIR AND MAKEUP. ♡
HEY, THAT'S MY MAKEUP CASE!
IT'S REALLY EXPEN-SIVE.

DON'T WORRY. IT'S FINE.
I'LL DO YOUR MAKEUP. I KNOW ALL THE LATEST TRENDS! ♡
YOU'LL LOOK JUST LIKE YOU CAME OUT OF A MAGAZINE.
パサッ
CLICK

WE'LL SPREAD THIS ON HERE.
...
MOVE IT LIKE THIS.
そわそわ
SCRATCH, SCRATCH
...
AND WE'LL PUT THIS COL-OR RIGHT OVER HERE.
うずうずうず
SHUFFLE

HM?
コレ
WHAT THIS?
ちらっ
GLANCE
...

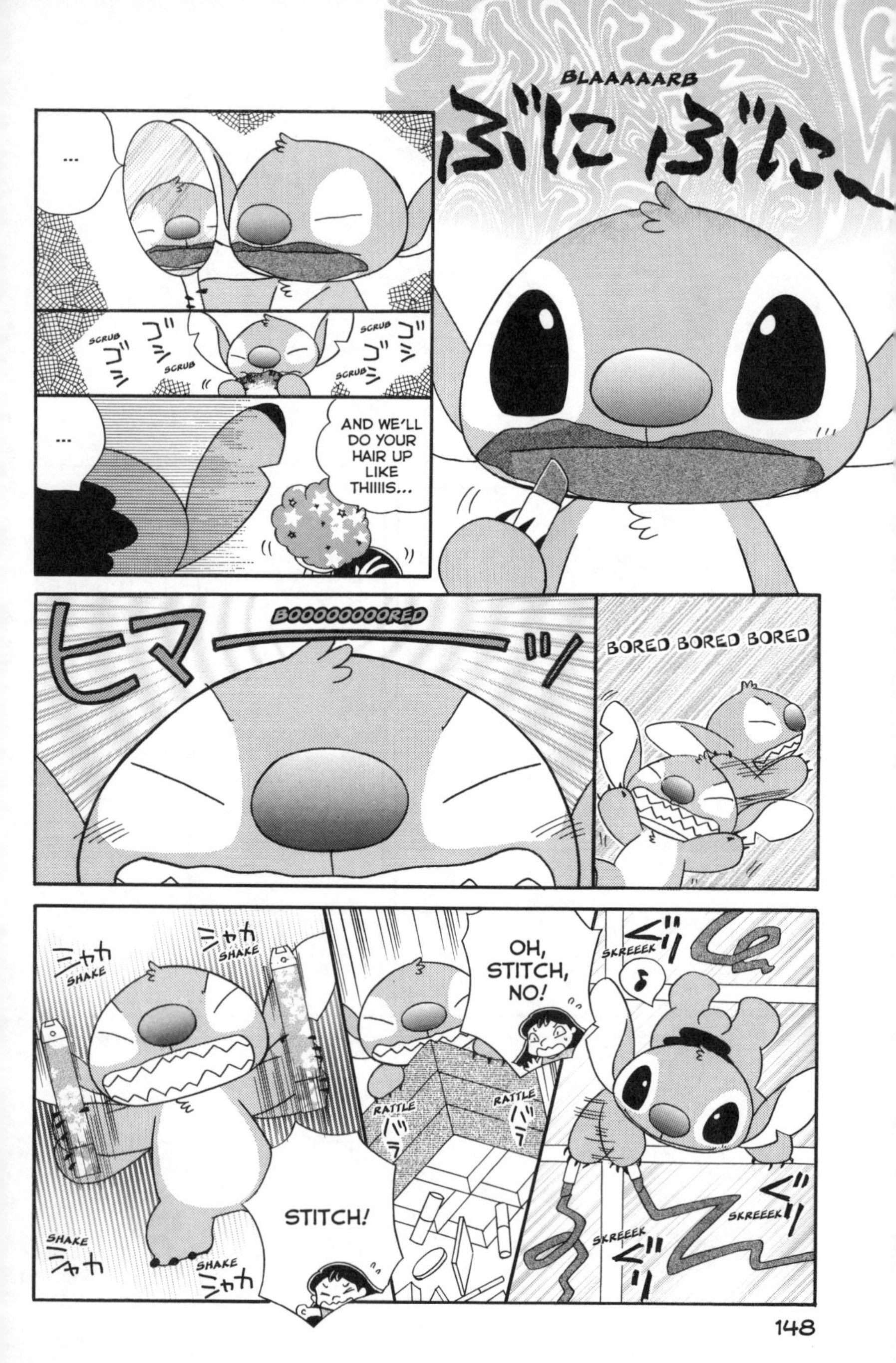
BLAAAAARB
ぶにぶにー
...
ゴシゴシ
SCRUB
SCRUB
ゴシゴシ
SCRUB
SCRUB
AND WE'LL DO YOUR HAIR UP LIKE THIIIIS...
...
BORED BORED BORED
BOOOOOOOORED
ヒマーーーッ
SKREEEK
ぐり
SKREEEK
ぐり
SKREEEK
ぐり
OH, STITCH, NO!
RATTLE
バラ
RATTLE
バラ
STITCH!
シャカ
SHAKE
シャカ
SHAKE
SHAKE
シャカ
SHAKE
シャカ

STITCH, WOULD YOU QUIET DOWN?
I'M DOING SOMETHING VERY IMPORTANT.
EGUEGH!
MONSTER!
うがーっ
GRAAAAAAAH
SPLOOSH
AAAAAAAAGH!
STOP IT, STITCH! THAT'S NANI!
プシュ
SPLOOSH
プシュ
SPLOOSH
SPLOOSH
プシュ
CUT IT OUT!
ACK! WHAT IS THIS?
STIIIITCH! PLEAK-LEEEEY!

HARUMPH! I'M EX-HAUSTED.
GOOD NIGHT.

STAAAAAARE
WHAT IS IT?? YOU'RE IN MY ROOM NOW, TOO?

YOU NEED TO SLEEP WELL FOR YOUR DATE TOMORROW!
WE'RE WATCHING OVER YOU SO YOU CAN GET TO SLEEP QUICKLY.
I CAN'T SLEEP LIKE THIS.

The next day…
GLARE
HUH?
YOU'RE SUP-POSED TO BE ON A FANCY CRUISE SHIP RIGHT NOW, RIGHT? WHY ARE YOU HERE?

I OVERSLEPT AND COMPLETELY MISSED MY DATE! IT'S ALL YOUR FAULT!
THIS IS HOW IT OPENED UP.
Mean-while, on the ship…
I WONDER IF SHE BROKE UP WITH ME.
SIIIGH
BWAAAAAH

TREASURE HUNTING AT THE BEACH!
Today is the Beach Treasure Hunt!
IN THESE CAPSULES, YOU'LL FIND NUMBERS FOR THE PRIZES ... FROM THE DOOR PRIZE ALL THE WAY TO THE GRAND PRIZE.
GOOD LUCK!
1
OKAY, TEAM, WE'RE LOOKING FOR THE GRAND PRIZE...A BRAND-NEW WASHING MACHINE!
RIGHT! WE'LL FIND IT!
Speak-ing of ...
WHAT DID YOU GUYS PUT IN THE WASHING MACHINE?!
NOW IT'S BROKEN!
ぷす
HISS
ぷす
HISS
NANI'S BEEN IN AN AWFUL MOOD EVER SINCE.
WE'LL JUST HAVE TO WIN THE GRAND PRIZE AND CHANGE HER MIND!
SIGH
RIGHT!

ピー
PIIII
READY... START!
わーーーっ
GOOOOO!
WOW, THERE ARE SO MANY PEOPLE!
LET'S START LOOKING!
AH, I FOUND ONE!
HERE, TOO! ♪
I GOT ONE, TOO!
WASHING MACHINE ...
WASHING MACHINE ...
WASHING MACHINE!
SHKT
SHKT
SHKT
パターーーッ
POP
POP
POP
GUM
GUM
GUM
THEY'RE ALL DOOR PRIZES ... CHEWING GUM!
BUMMER.
OOH!
PAT
PAT
PAT

ペタペタペタ~
PAT PAT PAT
...
じゃーーーん!
TADAAAAH!
EHE
WOOOW!
AMAZING!
ガオー
GRAOW
ガオー
GRAOW
ガオー
GRAOW
ガオー
GRAOW
ズシャア
SMASH
GRAOW
GRAOW
ズシャア
SMASH
WE'RE SCARED, MOMMY!
UWAAAAA
HEY YOU!
ぴゅ~
MRRRRRRAW

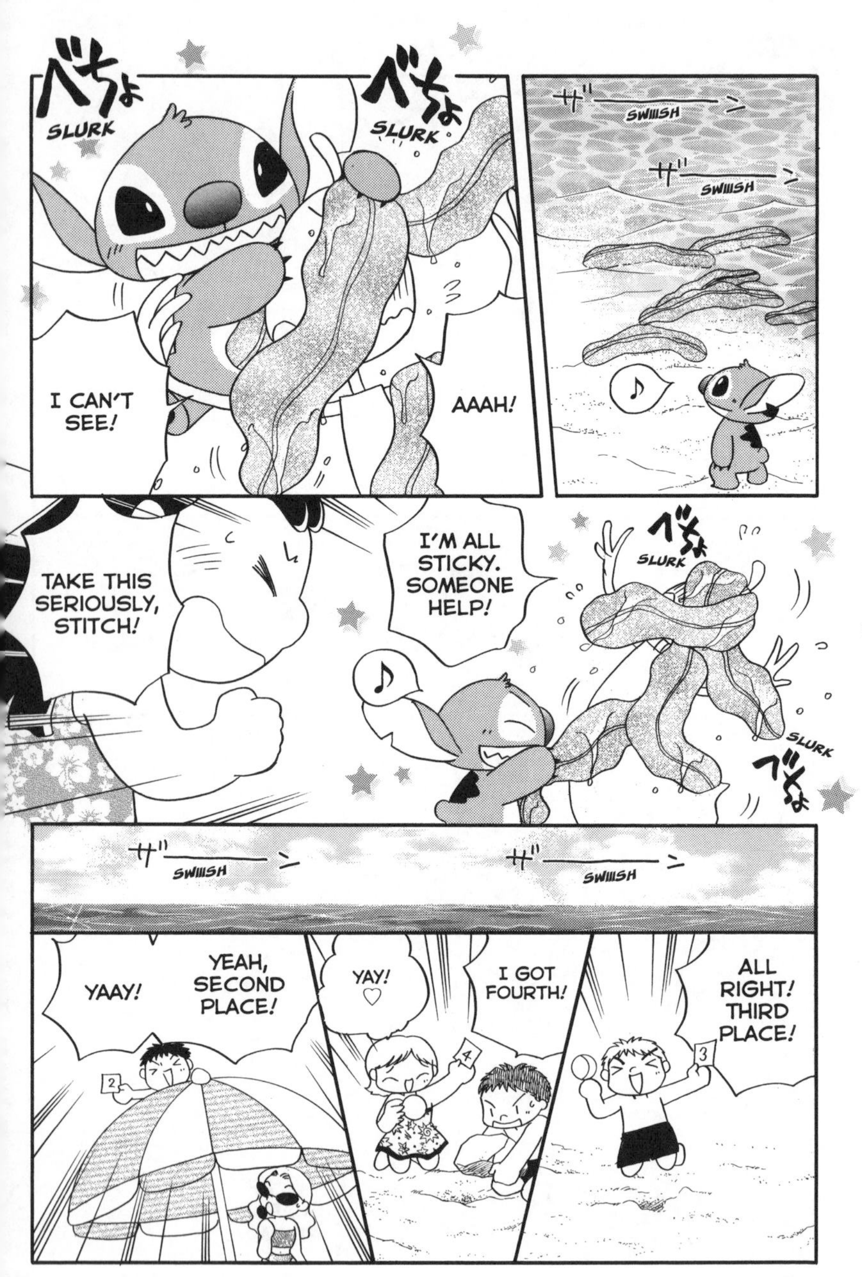
ザー
SWIIISH
ザー
SWIIISH
♪
べちょ
SLURK
AAAH!
べちょ
SLURK
I CAN'T SEE!
べちょ
SLURK
べちょ
SLURK
I'M ALL STICKY. SOMEONE HELP!
♪
TAKE THIS SERIOUSLY, STITCH!
ザー
SWIIISH
ザー
SWIIISH
ALL RIGHT! THIRD PLACE!
I GOT FOURTH!
YAY! ♡
YEAH, SECOND PLACE!
YAAY!

カァァァ…
SIZZLE
IT'S SO HOT, I CAN'T GO ON.
I'M FEELING DIZZY!
HAAH HAAH
WE'VE LOOKED EVERY-WHERE...
I HAVE TO KEEP LOOKING!
HAAH HAAH HAAH HAAH HAAH
SHKT
ざっざっ
...
HAAH HAAH HAAH HAAH
だっ
DASH
SCRAPE
する
SCRAPE
する
HEY STITCH, SETTLE DOWN AND CUT IT OUT!
ぼっ
THUD!

GRAB
ひょい
GRAB
ひょい
CHUCK
ブン
CHUCK
ブン
WHA? OW, OW!
ドゴン
CLUNG
ドゴン
CLUNG
STITCH!

ZIP!
AAAH!
WHAT ARE YOU DOING WITH MY STRAW?!
BADA!
バッ
YANK
LILO!
BING
DRINK TREE FRUIT!
AH!

YOU COULD TELL I WAS HOT AND EX-HAUSTED ... SO YOU GOT THIS FOR ME, DIDN'T YOU?
THANKS, STITCH!
STRAW HOLE!
POKE
パカーーーン!
BADADADAAAAH!
HEY!
THERE'S A CAP-SULE INSIDE!
OOH! LOOK, LOOK! ♡
WOW, IT'S THE GRAND PRIZE!
1
THEY HID IT IN THERE? GREAT JOB, STITCH!
THANKS!
ちゅっ♡
MMMWAH
OH, STITCH!

FIND SCRUMP!

Today's the day of the Beach Photo Contest!
Lilo's been looking forward to it but is down with a cold today.
THIS IS SCRUMP. SHE'S MY REALLY SPECIAL FRIEND.
YOU TAKE HER FOR ME.
ゲホ COUGH
ゲホ COUGH
OKAY! LILO!
SO YOU TAKE PICTURES AT THE BEACH, BUT YOU CAN ONLY SUBMIT ONE TO THE CONTEST.
GOOD LUCK, STITCH! ♡
FOR LILO!
DO BEST!
HEEEY, SO THAT WEIRD DOG FROM LILO'S PLACE IS JOINING, TOO.
MERTLE!

READ THIS WAY
I'M ALSO GOING TO ENTER WITH MY TOP-OF-THE-LINE CAMERA.
Lilo's frenemy, Mertle, and her dog, Gigi…
WELL, GOOD LUCK TAKING YOUR BIZARRE PICTURES, WEIRD LITTLE DOGGY.
SNORT
ムカー
GROOOWL
DON'T LOSE TO THAT LIT-TLE BRAT, STITCH!
DON'T CAUSE ANY TROUBLE!
だー
DASH
パシャッ☆
SNAP
YOU'RE HEAVY! MOVE IT!
ZZZZ
パシャ☆
SNAP
AAH!
FUNNY!
パシャッ☆
SNAP
ZIP
AAH! MY JUICE!

GO FOR IT, STITCH!
WHAT?
HUH...? GONE??
AAAGH!
WHAT TO DO?
GONE
GONE
GONE
YOU LOST SCRUMP?!
SORRY, LILO.
DIDN'T I TELL YOU THAT SCRUMP IS A REALLY SPE-CIAL FRIEND TO ME?
DON'T COME BACK UNTIL YOU FIND HER!
ゲホ
COUGH
ゲホ
COUGH
COUGH
ゲホ
ゲホ

BANG!
バタン!
IT'S NOT LIKE HE LOST HER ON PURPOSE.
RIGHT! SHE DIDN'T NEED TO BE THAT HARSH.
しゅん…
MMRRRR
YANK
べろん
AAAH!
HEY!
GRAUGH!
ガバァ
WAAAH!
ざしゅ
DIG
ざしゅ
DIG
ざしゅ
DIG
AH!
ザー
SWIIISH
ザー
SWIIISH
ぷか
BOB
ぷか
BOB
SCRUMP!
SPLASH
ざぶ
SPLASH
ざぶ

ざっぱーん
SPLOOOOOOSH
PLUNK
OH NO, HE WAS SWALLOWED UP BY THE WAVE!
HE'S TOO HEAVY TO COME BACK UP!
STITCH IS GONNA DROWN!

IS STITCH REALLY SINK-ING IN THE OCEAN?
HAAH
HAAH
HAAH
LILO!
COUGH
COUGH

WELL, HE WAS CHASING AFTER SCRUMP AND GOT SWALLOWED UP BY A WAVE.
NO, THAT'S AWFUL!
STITCH!
COUGH ゲホ
STITCH!
COUGH ゲホ
SWIIISH
WHAT SHOULD WE DO, JUMBA?
WE DON'T HAVE A SUBMARINE.
UNFORTUNATELY, WE NEED SOMETHING LIKE THAT.
IT'D TAKE ME TWO OR THREE DAYS TO MAKE ONE, TOO.
I'LL GO UNDER AND LOOK FOR HIM!
YOU CAN'T. YOU HAVE A COLD, AND YOU CAN BARELY EVEN WALK!
I'M FINE!
STITCH MUST BE EVEN WORSE OFF!
COUGH
COUGH
COUGH
HOLD ON, STITCH!

...
COUGH
COUGH
COUGH
COUGH
CALM DOWN! STITCH IS HERE.
....
ひょこっ
SHUDDER
JUMBA WENT TO GO SAVE HIM.
STITCH!
SORRY, LILO.
NOT SCRUMP!
SPECIAL FRIEND... GONE.
AWW!
SORRY.
OH, STITCH!
がばぁ!
GLOMP
I'M SO RELIEVED!

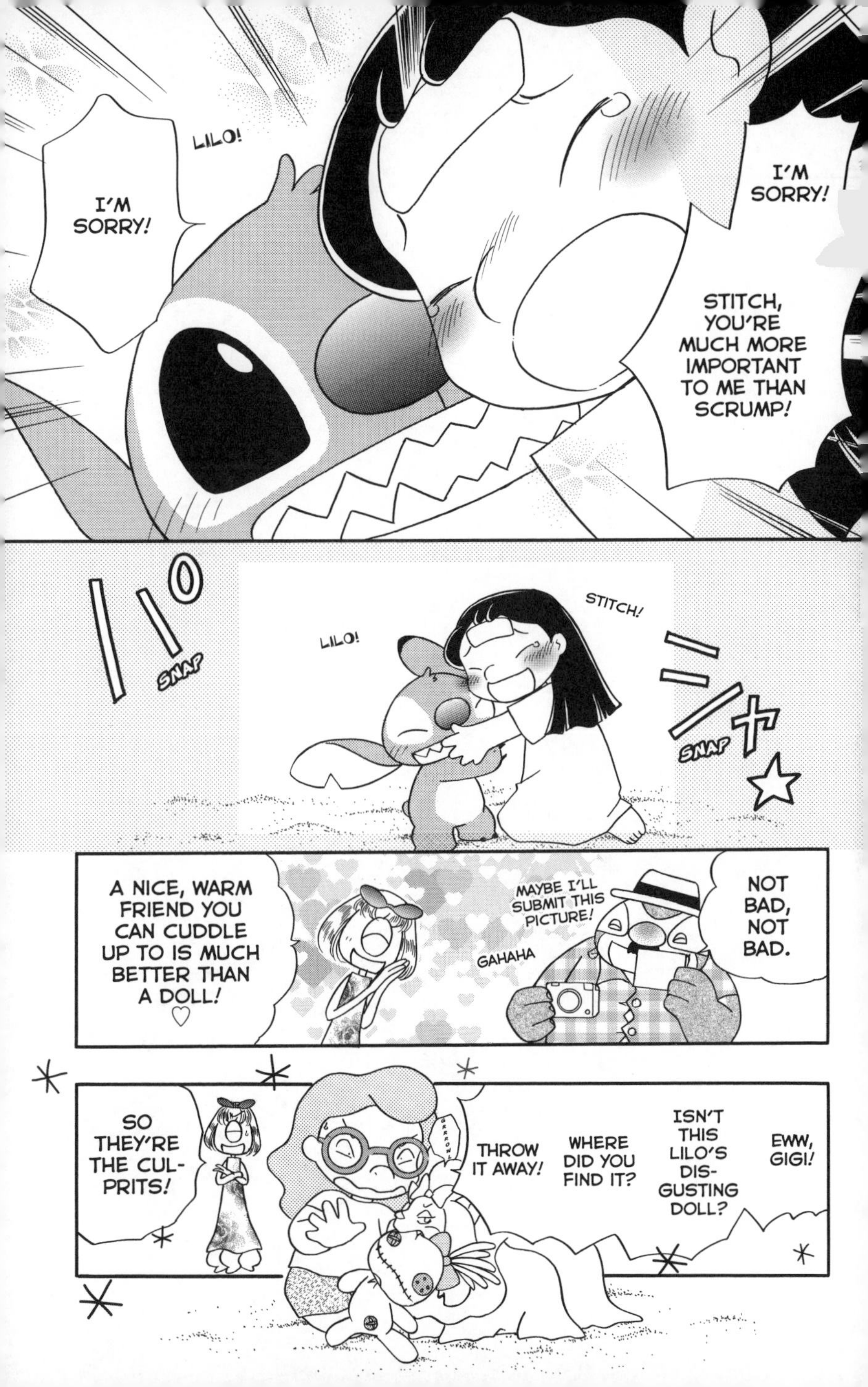
I'M SORRY!
STITCH, YOU'RE MUCH MORE IMPORTANT TO ME THAN SCRUMP!
LILO!
I'M SORRY!
STITCH!
LILO!
SNAP
SNAP
NOT BAD, NOT BAD.
MAYBE I'LL SUBMIT THIS PICTURE!
GAHAHA
A NICE, WARM FRIEND YOU CAN CUDDLE UP TO IS MUCH BETTER THAN A DOLL! ♡
EWW, GIGI!
ISN'T THIS LILO'S DIS-GUSTING DOLL?
WHERE DID YOU FIND IT?
THROW IT AWAY!
SO THEY'RE THE CUL-PRITS!

HM?

SEED OF THE HAPPINESS FLOWER

FIRST THING'S FIRST. BURY IT IN SOME SOFT SOIL AND GIVE IT SOME WATER!
ACK, CUT IT OUT, STITCH!
WAAATER
WAAATER
SPLOOSH
SPLOOSH
IT'S SPROUTING!
ONCE IT SPROUTS, BE SURE TO WATER IT EVERY DAY!
CHEW
CHEW
WHEN IT GETS BIGGER, GIVE IT SOME FERTILIZER.
SHAKE
SHAKE
AAAH!
STOP IT!
PEW
PEW
PEW

I HOPE IT'LL BLOOM SOON.
SIGH
SIGH
I WONDER WHAT KIND OF FLOWER WILL BLOOM.
ISN'T IT BORING DOING THIS EVERY DAY?
GAAAH!
GAAAH!

READ THIS WAY

SWISH
SWISH
BA!
SWISH
GAAH
CRASH!
AAH!

READ
THIS
WAY

STITCH, I CAN'T BELIEVE YOU!
AAAH... BUT THE STEM DIDN'T BREAK, SO IT'LL BE FINE IF YOU JUST REPLANT IT.
SORRY, LILO.
HMPH! IT'LL BE ALL YOUR FAULT IF I DON'T BE-COME HAPPY, STITCH!
Three days later...
TA-DAAAAH!
HAHAHA! MINE WAS THE FIRST TO BLOOM!
NO WAY! OURS DOESN'T EVEN HAVE A SINGLE BUD.
WHY??
AUGH! THIS IS ALL STITCH'S FAULT! I'LL NEVER BE HAPPY!
...
WE WORKED TOGETHER AND DID OUR BEST TO GROW IT, TOO.

YOU KNOW.
DAVID!
IT'S OKAY, LILO.
AAAGH!
DON'T TAKE IT SO SERIOUSLY.
HM
YEAH.
I'M HAPPY!
THE FLOWER ISN'T BLOOMING BECAUSE YOU'RE ALREADY HAPPY. ♡
GLANCE キョロ GLANCE キョロ
HEY, WHERE'S STITCH?
I'M SORRY, STITCH.
HEY, THAT'S RIGHT! ♡
STITCH!
バタン! SLAM
STIIIITCH!

WOW, THE FLOWER!
IT'S BLOOMING?!
AH!
NO, THIS FLOWER IS MADE OF TISSUE.
PFFT
PFFT
OH!
HE DID THIS FOR ME?
HE'S MADE A FLOWER OUT OF TISSUE!
PFFT
PFFT
STITCH!
GLOMP
LILO!
TEEHEE, I REALLY AM HAPPY!
MWAH!
?
?
Y'KNOW, MINE IS BLOOMING.
DOES THAT MEAN I'M NOT HAPPY?!
GULP!

IN THE NEXT VOLUME OF

Disney STITCH!

You loved him in *Lilo* and *Stitch.* Now Stitch's Japanese adventures continue as he explores an island near Okinawa with his new friend, Yuna. Join Stitch as he learns to mow a lawn, attempts to babysit, and tries to become a Japanese ninja. His hilarious hijinks are literally out of this world!

Disney Stitch! Volume 1

Story and Art by: Yumi Tsukirino

Publishing Assistant - Janae Young
Translator - Jason Muell
Retouching and Lettering - Vibrraant Publishing Studio
Social Media - Michelle Klein-Hass
Marketing - Kae Winters
Graphic Designer - Monalisa De Asis
Editor - Julie Taylor
Editor-in-Chief & Publisher - Stu Levy

TOKYOPOP Inc.
9420 Reseda Blvd Suite 555
Northridge, CA 91324

E-mail: info@TOKYOPOP.com
Come visit us online at www.TOKYOPOP.com

www.facebook.com/TOKYOPOP
www.twitter.com/TOKYOPOP
www.youtube.com/TOKYOPOPTV
www.pinterest.com/TOKYOPOP
www.instagram.com/TOKYOPOP
TOKYOPOP.tumblr.com

ISBN: 978-1-4278-5673-9

First TOKYOPOP printing: June 2016

10 9 8 7 6 5 4 3 2 1

Printed in China

This is the last page of the book!
You don't want to spoil the fun
and start with the end, do you?

In Japan, *manga* is created in accordance with the native language, which reads right-to-left when vertical. So, in order to stay true to the original, pretend you're in Japan -- just flip this book over and you're good to go!

Here's how:

If you're new to *manga*, don't worry, it's easy! Just start at the top right panel and read down and to the left, like in the picture here. Have fun and enjoy authentic *manga* from TOKYOPOP®!!